This book belongs to

_____

_____

_____

KT-161-821

MY Treasury OF ANIMAL STORIES

This book was created by Zigzag Publishing,
an imprint of Quadrillion Publishing Ltd.

Stories retold by Hazel Songhurst
Designed by Triggerfish
Design Manager Nicky Chapman
Editorial Manager Nicola Wright

Copyright © 1998 Quadrillion Publishing Ltd.
All rights reserved. No part of this publication may be reproduced,
stored in a retrieval system or transmitted in any form by any
means electronic, mechanical, photocopying or otherwise without
first obtaining written permission of the copyright owner.

This material first published by Quadrillion Publishing Ltd., under
the titles *Little Farmyard Adventures*, *Little Puppy Adventures*, *Little
Kitten Adventures*, *Little Pony Adventures*, *Little Bunny Adventures*,
Rocky Racoon and Friends

This edition published in 1998 by Colour Library Direct,
Godalming Business Centre, Woolsack Way, Godalming,
Surrey GU7 1XW.

ISBN 1-84100-006-X
Ref No 8574
Printed and bound in India

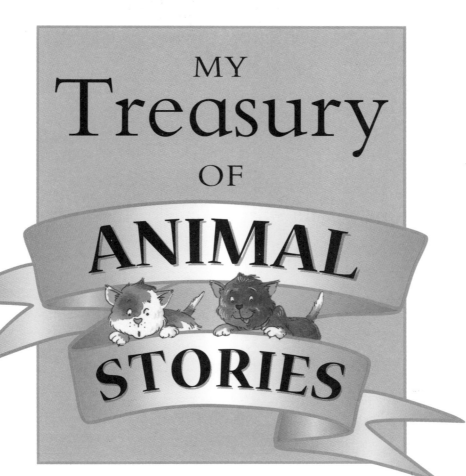

MY Treasury OF ANIMAL STORIES

Colour Library Direct

Contents

CHAPTER ONE

Kittens

Little Kitten Capers

Four unhappy little kittens press their noses against the window.

"I am bored playing chase with a silly ball of wool," grumbles Oscar.

"Me too!" miaows Rufus and he sighs.
Sleepy Lullaby, the youngest kitten, simply
opens her mouth wide in a big yawn. Veda, the
oldest kitten, is quiet. She is trying to think of an
exciting game they can all play.

   "I know!" she says. "Let's play follow the leader!"

Veda scampers away and the other kittens follow. She runs into the kitchen and squeezes inside a tiny cupboard full of tins and packets. But the cupboard is too small for the others to be able to follow. Veda knocks over a bag of flour. It spills everywhere!

"Oops," she says, as the white powder floats over Rufus, Oscar and Lullaby and settles on to the floor.

"Wow! What a mess," says Rufus.

"Atishoo!" sneezes Lullaby.

"Quick," says Oscar. "Follow me!"

The kittens shake themselves and follow Oscar. They leave a trail of little white paw-prints behind them as they run up the stairs and into the bathroom.

"Up here!" says Oscar as he leaps on to the shelf. Then, before the others can follow, his swinging tail knocks over a bottle of bubble bath.

"Oops!" says Oscar as the sticky, pink mixture pours out, making sweet-smelling soapy bubbles. Soon the bathroom is filled with floating pink bubbles.

"Shall we try to catch them all?" asks Lullaby.

"No," says Rufus. "Just follow me!"

In the hall, Rufus stops when he sees the skateboard.

"Come on kittens. Let's go for a ride," he says.
The excited kittens jump on at once and Rufus
pushes the skateboard from behind. They hold on
tightly as they zoom along the polished floor, going
faster and faster. Lullaby is wondering how they will
stop when – bump! – they hit the edge of the rug.

The skateboard turns over and the kittens tumble off.

"Ouch!" says Oscar rubbing his head. "That hurts."
The other kittens are rolling over and over on the
rug. Lullaby is pleased that they have stopped.

"Shall we do it again?" asks Rufus.

Suddenly, the kittens hear a voice they know well. They look up and see Mother Cat. Next to her is a broom, a floor mop and a bucket of soapy water.

"What a lot of mess you have all made!" she says. "Now it's time to play a new game. It's called the 'Tidying-up Game'!"

Little Kittens and the Big Cats

Mother Cat is watching her kittens as they cross the road. When they are sure no cars are coming, the little kittens walk carefully across the road.

The kittens are going to the zoo to see the big cats. Mother Cat has told them about their big cousins and now they are going to visit them! The little kittens are very excited as they scamper in through the gates.

"Look, there is a lion," says Veda. "Mother says he is King of the Jungle." The lion smiles at him.

"I wish I had a mane of hair like that," says Oscar fluffing up the fur around his face.

"I wish I was as big as a lion," says Rufus, standing straight and tall and puffing out his chest.

"Can we go?" asks Lullaby.

Lion

Oscar and Lullaby have found the tiger's den. The tiger doesn't mind when Veda sits on her back. It is feeding time at the zoo and she is busy eating her dinner. Then she growls loudly and Rufus is frightened. It makes the fur on his back stand up.

"I wish I could growl like that," says Oscar. He takes a deep breath and opens his mouth wide – but instead of growling fiercely, he just gives a loud miaow! Lullaby thinks this is very funny and she cannot stop laughing.

At first the kittens cannot see the big
spotted leopard lying lazily along a
branch high in a tree.

"There he is!" says Veda, pointing up.

The leopard is slowly swishing his
long, long tail backwards and forwards
as he looks down curiously at the little
kittens playing around his tree.

Oscar tries to climb the tree to get a
closer look at the leopard, but slides down.
"I wish my tail was longer," says Lullaby. She
runs round and round in circles, trying to catch
her tail. This makes her feel very dizzy.
"You're making the leopard feel dizzy, too,"
says Rufus, smiling.

Leopard

Now it is time for the little kittens to go home.

"Where is Oscar?" Lullaby asks Veda and Rufus. "Did he stay behind to talk to the leopard?" For a long time, the kittens search and call Oscar's name. At last, from somewhere high above their heads, they hear a faint growl. Veda, Rufus and Lullaby look up. There is Oscar, stretched out along a high branch. He is lazily swinging his tail backwards and forwards. "Come down," they shout. "It is feeding time at home."

Little Kittens in the Dark

"Veda, Oscar, Rufus, Lullaby!" calls Mother Cat. The sun is beginning to set and soon it will be dark. Mother Cat is worried about her little kittens. They are playing in the woods and really should have come home a long time ago.

"I'm sure they are safe," says Sally Squirrel, who is also worried about her friends. "I have an idea. You wait here and I will go and look for them," she says.

The little kittens are having lots of fun exploring the
woods. They do not notice that the shadows are
getting longer and that the sun is beginning to go
down. It is only when they hear Old Owl hoot and
then meet Bill Badger coming out of his sett, that
they realise it must be getting close to night-time.

"It is getting dark. We want to go home," miaow
Rufus, Lullaby and Oscar.

Veda is the oldest kitten and usually looks after the
others. She looks for the path that will take them
home. But she does not know which way to go.

"I think we are lost," she says, sadly.

The frightened kittens go along a winding path. It takes them out of the woods but leads into a big wheat field. The wheat stalks are so tall that even when Veda stands on Oscar and Rufus climbs up on Veda, the kittens cannot see above them.

Suddenly, they hear a loud, rustling sound coming from among the wheat stalks. Frightened rabbits and nervous field mice scurry to their safe nests. The kittens can see well in the dark, but they are too scared to look and see what is coming towards them!

"I've found you at last!" says a familiar voice. The kittens are delighted to see Sally Squirrel smiling at them from among the wheat stalks.

"How did you know where to find us?" asks Veda.

"Old Owl and Bill Badger showed me which path you took," answers Sally.

"We have been so frightened. Can you take us home now?" miaow the kittens.

The little kittens follow Sally through the dark woods. Old Owl flies across the fields, hooting loudly to tell all the animals that the kittens are safe. At last, in the distance the kittens see their home. The windows are glowing with light and Mother Cat is sitting on the wall, anxiously waiting for them.

Led by Sally Squirrel, Veda, Oscar, Rufus
and Lullaby race across the field as fast as they can.
Mother Cat hugs each one of them and Oscar asks,
"May we explore the woods again tomorrow?"
Can you guess what the other kittens
reply?

Little Kittens Make a Friend

One day, the little kittens are playing in the garden when a strange box is carried out and placed on the grass. It is made of wood and covered with wire.

When they look inside, they see a little blue house, a small red bowl and lots of straw.

"What sort of home is this?" whispers Lullaby.

Just as the kittens' noses touch the wire, a small furry creature scuttles towards them from the back of the cage. The frightened kittens scatter! Oscar, Veda and Rufus climb up the tree. Lullaby tries to follow, but she is not very good at climbing. Instead she hides behind the tree trunk and peeks out.

"What is it?" asks Lullaby, trembling.

"I think it looks quite friendly," says Oscar.

"But what is it doing here in our garden?" asks Veda. "Come on. Let's go and find out."

Slowly the kittens creep towards the box.

"Hello!" says the creature. "I want to come out and play. Can you please open the door to my cage?" Veda is the only one of the kittens who is brave enough to do it. She takes a deep breath and creeps slowly toward the cage on her tummy. Then, with a flick of her paw, she opens the door. The brown furry animal scuttles out and smiles at the kittens.

"Thank you for letting me out," he says.

"My name is Pepe and I am a guinea pig. Now,
what game do you think we should all play?"
The little kittens have never seen a guinea pig before.

It is fun to have a new friend to play with but the kittens have no idea what a guinea pig can do. The curious kittens have lots of questions to ask.

"Can you catch butterflies?" asks Oscar.

"No," says Pepe. "I can't run and jump like you."

"Can you miaow and purr?" asks Veda.

"No," says Pepe. "I can only squeak. Listen to this. Eek! Eek! Eek!"

The squeaking is so loud that the kittens have to put their paws over their ears.

"What games can you play?" asks Rufus.

"I can play Hide-and-Seek. Do you want to play?"

"Yes please!" say the kittens excitedly.

Hide-and-Seek is the kittens' favourite game of all.

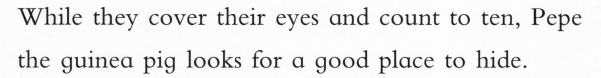

While they cover their eyes and count to ten, Pepe
the guinea pig looks for a good place to hide.

"... nine, ten," calls Veda. "Coming – ready or not!"
The kittens search everywhere – under the bushes,
behind the tree, even inside the empty flower pot...but
they can't find him anywhere! Look very carefully.
Can you see where Pepe is hiding?

CHAPTER TWO

Puppies

At the Seaside

One hot, sunny day Biscuit, Bella, Tansy and Zack went on a trip to the seaside. The puppies had never seen the sea before and they were all very excited.

The beach was enormous and seemed to stretch for miles. Bella and Tansy rushed to the edge of the sea and began to chase each other up and down. They left paw prints in the damp sand behind them. Biscuit wagged her tail and barked excitedly at the waves.

Zack was busy digging a great big hole in the sand.

"I might find some buried treasure left behind by a pirate if I dig deep enough," he thought to himself. But although he dug deeper and deeper, all he found was more and more sand.

Biscuit went down to the water's edge and looked at the sea. Little waves splashed gently on to the beach at his feet and he tried to catch them. He was feeling hot and thirsty and he drank some sea water.

"Ugh!" he spluttered. "It tastes salty – horrible!"

Meanwhile, Zack had gone right into the water and was trying his best to swim.

"Look at me! I'm swimming!" he called to the others. "This is just how Freda Frog does it. I wish she was here to see," he said.

Tansy and Bella had gone exploring along the beach. Suddenly they saw a strange creature walking towards them. It had six legs, two sharp-looking claws and an angry face. They had never seen anything like it before and they sniffed it curiously.

"Go away!" said the grumpy crab. "This is my part of the beach!" and he waved his claws at them.

For the rest of the day, the puppies played on the beach. When it was time to go home, everyone felt very tired. They had all had great fun and they felt very sad that the sunny day was over.

"What a pity we can't stay longer," said Bella.

"I've found these beautiful sea shells," said Biscuit.

"If we take them home they will remind us of our happy sunny day at the seaside."

Lost and Found

One day, Tansy and Biscuit decided to go for a walk in the woods. Their best friend Sidney Squirrel asked if he could come too. As Tansy and Biscuit strolled along, Sidney ran quickly ahead. He loved climbing the trees and playing hide-and-seek in the branches.

Suddenly, they heard a strange sound coming from nearby. The puppies pricked up their ears to listen.

"What's that noise?" said Biscuit. "It's not a happy sound. It sounds exactly like someone crying!"

Sitting under a tree were two little children. They
were hugging each other and they looked very sad.

"We're lost," they said. "We were having a picnic
with Mum and Dad, and we went to play hide-and-
seek. Now we can't find our way back."

Tansy and Biscuit ran straight over to the children.

"Don't worry," said Biscuit. "We can help you find them. Please don't cry any more." Biscuit had thought of a clever plan. There was a very tall tree nearby and he asked Sidney to climb all the way to the very top of it.

Sidney scurried up the tree as fast as he could. When
he got to the top, he held on tightly to a branch.
From here, Sidney could see right across the woods.

"It's all right! I can see your parents," he called
down at last. "They're not far away."

As the woodland animals watched, the puppies led the happy children through the trees.

"Thank you for helping us," said the children.

"It is easy to get lost here," Tansy explained. "It is always best not to wander from the path."

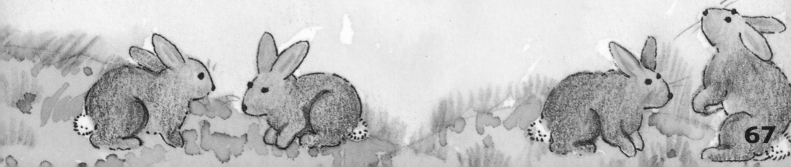

The children's parents hugged and kissed them. They were very happy and relieved to see them again.

"Whatever happened to you? We were so worried." they said. And the children told them everything.

"Thank goodness these clever puppies found you!"

As a reward for their good work, Tansy and Biscuit were allowed to share the children's picnic. There was even some fruit for Sidney to enjoy! Before saying goodbye, they played one last game of hide-and-seek – and this time nobody got lost!

Nobody Wants to Play

Zack was bored with playing ball in the garden by himself. He found Biscuit in the kitchen and asked him if he wanted to come outside and play.

"Come on, Biscuit," he said. "It'll be fun!"

"Not now," said Biscuit. "I'm eating my breakfast!"

In the corner of the kitchen, Bella and Tansy were curled up in bed. Zack woke them up.

"Don't just lay there snoozing!" he barked. "You're missing all the fun. Come outside and play!"

"Not now," said Bella with a yawn. "We're much too tired. You'd better come back later."

"Yes, when we're awake," said sleepy Tansy.

Poor Zack! He decided to go and look for Freda Frog in her pond in the garden.

"Perhaps Freda wants to play," he thought. Freda was sitting quietly on a lily pad. She did not seem to be doing anything important.

"Will you come and play with me?" he asked. But Freda said she was just too busy looking for flies.

Sidney Squirrel had been watching. He looked down at Zack from the branch of a tree.

"Before you ask," he said, "I'm afraid that I'm busy counting nuts, so I can't come and play either. If I were you, I would look for something useful to do."

But Zack did not want to do anything useful. He wanted to have fun and play with his friends.

Zack picked up his ball and walked slowly to the
other end of the garden. He lay down on the lawn
and put his head on his paws. He was feeling very
sad and lonely.

"Why won't anyone play with me?" he thought.
"What did I do? Don't they like me any more?"

Zack was just wondering whether he should run away from home when Bella and Biscuit came scampering up, with Tansy not far behind them. When he saw this, Sidney ran down from his tree and Freda hopped right out of the pond.

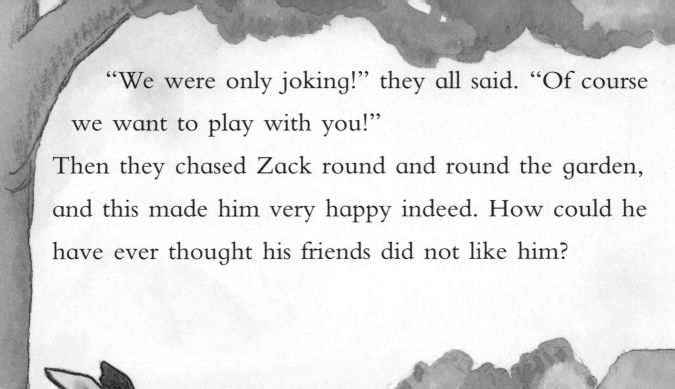

"We were only joking!" they all said. "Of course we want to play with you!"

Then they chased Zack round and round the garden, and this made him very happy indeed. How could he have ever thought his friends did not like him?

Treasure Hunt

"I need your help," said Sidney to Tansy. "I buried a store of nuts in the garden, but now I can't remember where they are. Please help me find them."

Tansy was more than happy to help. She loved digging. To begin with, she decided to dig a few small holes in the vegetable garden where the cabbages were growing. She worked hard but she couldn't find any hidden nuts.

"I'd better try somewhere else," she thought.

In the onion patch she dug one very big hole. But, though she dug deeper and deeper, there was still no sign of Sidney's nut store.

Zack saw what was going on and decided to join in the hunt. He thought it would be a good idea to try the flower bed. He scratched around in the soil and some of the flowers got broken and trampled.

Meanwhile, Bella decided to join in. She thought she would try the lawn. It was hard work making even a small hole in the grass and Bella had to dig in several different places before she made a good start.

Tansy, Zack and Bella worked hard at their digging.
Sidney watched carefully for any sign of the nuts.
Then Biscuit came along. When he saw what the
other puppies had done to the garden, he was
very annoyed.

"Look at the mess you have made!" he cried.

The puppies were ashamed of themselves. They did their best to tidy up the mess before anyone else saw what they had done. Biscuit replaced the grass and Tansy and Bella put back the vegetables. Zack even tried to mend some of the broken flowers.

While this was going on, Sidney sat still
and looked thoughtful.

"Oh no!" he said, "I've just remembered. I buried
those nuts in the woods, not in the garden!"

And he ran off to find them for himself.

CHAPTER THREE

Bunnies

Bunnies' Snow Search

"Brrrr, I'm freezing," said Heather as the little bunnies made their way home across the field.

"It is very cold," said Violet. "Wait a minute, what's this on my nose? I can't quite see."

"I think it's called a snowflake," answered William. "I've never seen snow before."

The bunnies stared in amazement as the falling snow formed a white blanket over the ground.

"It feels so soft," said William.

"Let's have some fun!" shouted Basil. And he began to roll and play in the snow.

"Look at this!" cried Heather as she kicked up a spray of snow which covered William from his ears to his tail.

"A snow bunny, " giggled Violet.

The bunnies rolled around and around in the snow laughing and giggling with delight. It was a very long time before they managed to stop!

At last the bunnies got their breath back. To their surprise the snow was still falling fast.

"Will it last forever?" sighed Violet.

"I hope not, or we will never find our way home," grumbled Heather. The little bunnies looked around and saw that their path home had disappeared.

"What are we going to do?" said Violet. "We shouldn't have stayed out so long!"

"What's that noise?" cried Basil staring upwards. The other bunnies looked into the sky and saw their friends Marianne and Michael coming in to land.

"Hello little bunnies," said the kind geese. "Can we help you to find your way home? Just follow us." With the help of their friends, the little bunnies reached the edge of the garden. But as they pushed their little noses through the hedges, they saw a large stranger looming over them!

"Who's that in our garden?" squeaked Violet.

"He looks frightening!" wailed William.

"Don't worry," laughed Michael. "I've met his type before. He's called a snowman, and he's not the tiniest bit scary!"

The bunnies soon got over their fright when they realised the stranger was only made of snow!

As the bunnies hopped across the snowy lawn towards their hutch, they noticed strange footprints leading to the open door.

"Who's that in our hutch?" said William.

"Good afternoon," called a small muffled voice. There was a rustle and a snuffle, and from under the pile of straw appeared the face of the bunnies' old friend Morris Mole!

"Just keeping the hutch warm for you," he explained. The tired little bunnies did not mind this in the least. Before long, they snuggled down too and were soon feeling cosy and warm. They fell fast asleep and dreamed of softly falling snowflakes.

Bunnies in Clover

One morning, the little bunnies were nibbling at the short green grass in their run in the garden.

But Basil had other things on his mind. He hopped towards the door of the run.

"Mmmm, that clover looks delicious," he said, twitching his little nose. "It's a shame we can't reach it," he muttered as he leaned against the door.

Snap – the door suddenly sprang open and out rolled Basil onto the garden path. The three other bunnies ran over at once and pushed their heads out through the open door.

"Are you okay, Basil?" asked Heather.

"Is it safe out there?" asked Violet.

"Don't be silly!" laughed Basil. "This is our chance to eat some yummy clover."

The four little bunnies hopped one after the other across the garden, their fluffy white tails bobbing up and down behind them. They couldn't wait to find some delicious clover to eat.

The bunnies soon found a thick patch of clover and had just settled down for a tasty feast when the earth beneath them started to quiver. Violet felt scared. "Help! What is happening?" she asked. "Is there going to be an earthquake?"

The bunnies could see that dirt was flying in all directions and something was moving under the ground. The mound of dirt grew larger and moved more and more. Then out popped a little black snout followed by two large paws, looking just like shovels.

The bunnies all laughed when they saw their old friend Morris Mole climbing out from underneath the pile of dirt.

"Good morning, bunnies. Good morning," he said. Then he looked around him in surprise. "Oh dear! I think I have tunnelled too far – I'd planned to come out on the edge of the woods!"

"What are the woods?" asked
William, curiously.

"Don't you know what the woods are?" said Basil.

"Why don't you all come with me?" said Morris,

"And then I can show you the woods."

"Is there lots of clover in the woods?" asked Basil. "I hope so. We all love clover!"

"You can find clover all over the woods," said Morris. "And I can take you to the special glade I know, where the tastiest clover of all grows."

With Morris leading the way, the little bunnies hopped out of the garden and into the woods. The bunnies spent the afternoon in the special glade, filling their little tummies with clover while Morris tunneled his way around them.

"That was the best clover I've ever tasted," sighed Basil, as they all fell into a happy sleep.

Bunnies to the Rescue

The bunnies had spent the day playing in the woods.
"Shouldn't we be going home by now?" Violet
asked the other little bunnies as they played leapfrog.
"Hurry up, it's starting to get dark," said William.

Suddenly they heard a very loud noise. It stopped them in their tracks.

"Whooo, Whooo, Whooo, Whooooaaah!"

What a spooky sound! The bunnies felt quite scared.

A large black shadow flew over the bunnies, heading towards a tall tree in front of them.

Crash, bump, slither! The shadow collided with the tree, making the bunnies jump back in fright.

"Look out!" cried Heather. "What was that?"

A crumpled old owl slid down the tree trunk and landed in a heap at the little bunnies' feet.

"Ooh, my head," moaned the poor hurt owl.

The little bunnies could see something was wrong.

When they little realised that the scary black shadow

was only an old owl they stopped feeling afraid.

"Are you alright?" asked Heather. "You hit the tree with a terrible bang."

"I think so," said the owl, whose name was Horatio. "I'm getting used to bumping into things."

I haven't been able to fly properly ever since this horrible string got caught around my wing."

"Oh dear," said Violet, sympathetically. "It must make it very difficult for you to get around."

"I can help you with that," said William, who
started to nibble away at the tough string. He worked
very hard and after what seemed like a long time, his
little sharp teeth finally broke the string.

"I've done it!" he said.

With a happy sign, Horatio stretched out his wing as far as it would go.

"That feels so much better," he hooted happily. "I must think of a good way to thank you all!"

"Could you show us the way out of the woods?" asked Violet. "We're lost."

"I'd be delighted to help," answered Horatio. "I know these woods better than any other animal. Follow me!" And he flew up in to the air.

Horatio's wing was now as good as new. The little bunnies had to run very fast to keep up with him. Soon they reached the edge of the woods.

From the top of the hill the little bunnies could see
their garden. Their cosy hutch was lit up by the
bright moonlight and it looked warm and inviting.

"Thank you Horatio!" they called to their friend.

"Come and visit me again soon," hooted Horatio.
And he disappeared into the night sky with a
sweeping wave of his wing.

Bunnies Make a Splash

Early one morning, the little bunnies hopped down to the bottom of the hill and came to a large pond.

They had never seen so much water before!

"It looks very cold and very deep," said Violet, as they crept to the edge of the pond and peered down.

"Look at this!" cried Basil. "There is another bunny in the water. He looks exactly like me!"

"Don't be silly," said Heather. "That's not another bunny, it's just your reflection."

"It's my what?" asked Basil in a puzzled voice.
He decided to take a closer look. As he leaned
further forward, he lost his balance and then rolled
nose first into the water – plop!

"Basil's fallen in to the pond!" shouted Heather.

Luckily for Basil, the pond was not deep and he
could easily stand up in the water. But he was a very
wet and unhappy little bunny. Not only did he have
water in his ears but he couldn't move! His paws had
got stuck in the mud at the bottom of the pond.

"Help!" he cried. "Please get me out!"

As the little bunnies stood helplessly at the side of the pond, two long necks appeared out of the mist.

"Can we help?" asked two kind geese. Their names were Marianne and Michael.

"I am cold and I am wet and I am stuck," moaned Basil. "I want to get out of here!"
The two geese swam up right next to Basil, Marianne on one side and Michael on the other. Poor wet Basil felt quite nervous at this. Then the two geese scooped up the little bunny with their beaks and placed him back on dry land.

"Stupid pond!" said cross, wet Basil.

The geese looked fiercely down their beaks at him.

"Don't you know that little bunnies and cold ponds don't mix?" said Marianne.

"You have to be very careful near water!" Michael warned sternly.

Basil realised that he had behaved badly and he said
he was sorry to Marianne and Michael.

"Now, is there anything else we can do for you
all?" asked Marianne gently.

Heather was worried that Basil might catch cold.

"Yes, please," she said. "We need to reach the other side so Basil can get home to our warm hutch." So, the geese let the bunnies climb on their backs and carried them one by one safely across the pond.

CHAPTER FOUR

Ponies

Breaking the Ice

One cold, snowy morning, all the trees had icicles hanging from their branches.

"Brrr! It's chilly today," said Dora Duck as she came down to the pond for her daily swim. When she got there she was amazed to see that the water had frozen solid.

"Oh dear," she thought. "What shall I do? I wonder if the ponies can help me?"

"I've got an idea," said Cassie. "I can break the ice for you with my hoof."

"No!" barked Ralph the dog. "That would be very dangerous! You are too heavy and you might fall through the ice into the water."

Everyone stood and looked at the frozen water and wondered what they could do to help.

"I've had an idea," said Duchess, after a while.

"We can roll that big stone down the hill into the pond. It should make a hole in the ice."

Duchess and Cassie tried to move the heavy stone.
While Duchess scraped away the earth around it
with her hoof, Cassie pushed the stone with her nose.
It was very hard work. Cassie's nose was starting to
ache and she nearly gave up.

After a long time, the stone slowly began to move. Then it gathered speed and suddenly rolled fast down the hill. It fell into the pond and the ice broke with a loud SPLASH! Duchess felt very pleased that her clever plan had worked.

"You've done it!" cried Dora, dancing happily.

There was just enough room for a duck to have a quick dip. Now Dora could enjoy her swim after all, even if the water felt icy and cold!

"Thank you, everybody!" she quacked happily, as she jumped into the water.

Lucky Escape

The wind was howling in the treetops. It bent all the branches over and blew down the leaves.

Ted and Drummer found shelter under a big tree. But Ralph was enjoying himself – he loved windy days! The excited little dog ran up and down, chasing the leaves that were blowing around the field.

Poor Dora Duck was holding on to a tree. She didn't feel at all safe. She was very small and light, and she was sure that the strong wind might blow her away!

Suddenly, the wind grew even stronger and it howled even harder. Ralph thought he heard a faint creaking noise. It seemed to be coming from the big tree.

Ralph knew that something was badly wrong. He ran over to the tree for a closer look. Then he saw the big tree slowly start to move.

"Run!" he barked at the ponies as loudly as he could. "The tree is going to fall down!"

Ted and Drummer galloped away from under the tree as quickly as they could. Dora ran after them, flapping her wings. The ponies and the little duck escaped just in time. Crash! The tree was blown right over!

"What a lucky escape!" said Ted. "What a clever dog you are Ralph! Thank you for warning us."

"Look!" shouted Drummer. "Now we can have lots of fun jumping over the fallen tree trunk!"

While the ponies were playing, Ralph decided to bury one of his bones under the roots of the fallen tree. The wind was dying down. Feeling braver now, Dora set off for the safety of her pond.

Rainy Day Monster

It was a very rainy day. Poor, soaked Duchess was trying to find shelter by the hedge. Even Ralph hated getting wet. They were gloomily watching Dora as she danced and quacked and splashed in the mud.

Suddenly Drummer trotted up, looking worried.

"There's a monster coming up the hill," he said.

"It's horrible! It's all brown and green
and slimy-looking."

They all looked down the hill and saw the brown monster coming towards them.

"Do you think we should run away?" asked Ralph nervously. "Or is it best to just keep very still?"

As the monster got closer and closer, Drummer felt afraid and he tried to hide behind Duchess.

"I don't like it!" he said, trying not to cry.

"Don't worry," said Duchess. "It might be friendly."

The little ponies stayed still and quiet so as not to frighten the monster. It came right up to them and stopped and looked at each of them in turn. Drummer was scared and got farther behind Duchess.

"Hello. Who are you?" said Duchess bravely.

"It's only me," said the monster in a familar voice. Then everyone could see that it was – Cassie!

"I rolled in the mud and lots of it has stuck to me," she explained. "I didn't mean to get so dirty."

Everyone laughed. Drummer forgot he had ever been afraid and came out from his hiding place.

"We thought you were a monster!" he said.

"Don't worry about being dirty," said Duchess. "It's still raining hard. It will wash the mud away and you will soon look like Cassie again."

Thirsty Work

The sun was shining brightly on a beautiful summer's day. The little ponies were feeling hot.

"I'm thirsty," said Drummer to his friends. "Let's go down to the stream for a drink."

But, when the ponies got to the stream, they found that all the water had disappeared!

"What has happened?" wondered Ted. "Has the sunshine dried up the stream?"

The ponies decided to search along the bank of the stream. Soon they came to a place where the water was blocked by earth and twigs.

"No wonder the stream is dry!" said Duchess. "I wonder what we can do?" She thought hard.

"We need Ralph to help us," said Duchess at last.

"Here I am," said Ralph. "What seems to be the trouble? I'll help if I can."

"Our stream is blocked," Duchess explained. "There's a big mound of dirt in the way. Do you think you can clear it for us?"

"Oh, yes," barked Ralph. "That's easy. I can dig out all that dirt in no time at all."

Ralph went to work at once. Dirt started to fly up in the air as he started to dig away at the mound.

There were lots of twigs and leaves mixed up with the earth. Ralph asked Dora to help him.

"If you carry all these twigs away in your beak we'll be finished much sooner," he said.

Dora worked very hard, gathering up all the twigs.

Soon the stream was flowing freely again and the thirsty ponies could have a drink at last.

"Mmmm....delicious cool water," said Duchess.

"Thank you Ralph and Dora, for being so clever and working so hard!" said all the little ponies.

Ralph and Dora were feeling hot after all the digging and carrying they had done. They both jumped into the water and splashed around to cool off.

CHAPTER FIVE

Forest Friends

Rocky and Ricky

Rocky Racoon's cousin Ricky lives in the city. He has come to stay with Rocky for the weekend. Ricky has never visited a forest before.

"We'll play our favourite games," say the animals.

"This is the best tree for climbing," says Eddie the bear cub, scrambling up the big maple tree.

"Climbing trees is boring," says Ricky. "It's what stupid little kids do."

"But everyone likes climbing trees!" say the Squirrel sisters.

Rosie, Spike, Eddie and B.B.
decide to roll down the hill.

"This is fun! Come and play,
Ricky!" they shout.

"Not me. Rolling down hills is boring," says Ricky. "Hasn't anyone around here even got a skateboard?"

The big old moose gives everyone a ride.

"Can't you go any faster?" whines Ricky.

"Then it won't be so boring."

"Let's catch some fish
for dinner," says B.B. Beaver. He and Rosie
paddle off in the canoe.

"Fish are disgusting! Yuk! I only eat
fish sticks," says Ricky.

There are no more games to show Ricky. The forest friends feel disappointed that he doesn't want to play with them. They walk slowly along, trying to think of something to do that Ricky won't find boring.

"Oh, let's just go home early," says Eddie, sadly.

"What are those?" asks Ricky pointing at a bush.

"They're just boring old blueberries," says Rocky.

"Don't you have blueberries in the city?"

"Not like these," says Ricky, filling
his mouth with blueberries.
"These taste really yummy!"
And he eats more, and
more, and more!

That evening, Ricky eats blueberries for supper. The next day, he has blueberries for breakfast. Rocky's mum asks the animals to pick lots more blueberries. "Ricky's going back to the city tomorrow, so I've decided to cook blueberry pancakes for his goodbye dinner," she says.

"Do you think I could stay a few more days, Rocky?" asks Ricky, after he has finished six blueberry pancakes. "I think I've changed my mind about the forest — I really like it after all!"

Rocky and the Scarves

Brrr! It's a very cold snowy day. Rocky Racoon's mum has made him wear a woolly scarf.

"Promise me you will keep it on," she says.

Rocky meets Spike the porcupine. His mum has made him wear a scarf, too!

B.B. Beaver's mum has made B.B. wear his new blue scarf.

And Eddie the bear cub's mum made Eddie wear her own scarf.

And Rosie the skunk and the squirrel sisters are wearing warm, woolly scarves, too!

After a while, the forest friends all began to feel uncomfortable wearing their scarves.

"My mum said I that must not lose my scarf," says B.B. Beaver.

"So did my mum," says everyone else.

"I know how we can have
some fun," says Rocky. They take off their scarves
and Rocky shows them how to tie them together.

The long scarf-rope made a great swing.

"Wheee! I want to go higher!" shouts Rosie.

And a strong climbing rope.
"Now even I can climb up
trees!" says B.B. Beaver,
as Eddie pulls him up
the tree trunk.

The squirrel sisters teach
everyone their skipping games.

HEAVE! Which side will win the tug-of-war game?

"This is the best game of all," says Rocky. "Keep

pulling Spike and B.B.!"

The forest friends have had lots of
fun. Now it's time to go home.
  "Make sure everyone puts on the
right scarf," warns Rocky.
The animals sort out the
      tangle of scarves and
          everyone finds their own.

But something is wrong!
   "Oh well," they all
laugh. "At least we didn't
lose them!"

Eddie Gets Stuck

Eddie the bear cub is in big trouble! He loves to climb trees, and now he has climbed UP a big tree, but he can't climb DOWN.

"Poor Eddie," says Rosie. "He's stuck. How can we get him down from there?"

"I know," says Rocky. "Let's collect as many leaves as we can and make a big soft pile of them for Eddie to fall on."

The forest friends worked very hard and at last the pile was ready.

"Jump, Eddie!" they cried. "You'll be fine!"

"I I I c c can't!" stutters Eddie, closing his eyes and clinging on tightly to the branch. "I'm scared!"

"I'll go up and help him down," says Rocky. The others watch him climb up.

"I'm here, Eddie," says Rocky.
"Take my paw and we'll climb
down the tree together."

"I I I c c can't!" says Eddie.
"I'm much too frightened to move."

"I've got an
idea. If I gnaw
through the trunk, then the
tree will fall down," says B.B.
Beaver, excitedly.

"NO!" shouts Eddie. "That would be dangerous!"

"It's okay, Eddie," says Rocky. "I've got a plan."

"Oh well, it's time to go home
for dinner now," says Rocky
suddenly in a loud voice.

"Oh yes! So it is," say
the others. "Bye!"

But instead of going home, the forest friends hide
behind a nearby bush and peek through the leaves.

And can you guess what they see? They see Eddie move very slowly and start to climb back down the tree!

"I think I am feeling a bit hungry now," says Eddie as he gets halfway down the trunk. "Getting stuck in a tree must give you an appetite. I hope the others don't eat my share of dinner." And he reaches the ground.

"Wait for me!" he shouts.

"We were!" say the others, laughing.

"You're a better climber than you think,

Eddie!" says Rocky Racoon.

B.B.'s Monster

The forest friends are having fun rolling down a hill. B.B. Beaver is having the first turn. See how fast he goes...

...wheee! Bump, bump, bump, bump.

"It's my turn next," says Rosie Skunk,

jumping excitedly.

But before Rosie can start rolling, B.B.
comes running back up the hill.
He is waving his arms about
and shouting loudly.

"Help, help! Help, help!"
shouts B.B. in a very
frightened voice.

Poor B.B. is so out of breath
that he can hardly speak.

"There's a monster at the bottom of the hill!" he
says at last. "I've just seen it! It's huge and horrible!"
Brave Rocky isn't at all scared by this news.

"Let's go and
look!" says Rocky.

"What is it?" whispers Rosie, feeling scared.

"SHMEESHMIKE!" roars the horrible monster.

"Oh no!" tremble Eddie, Rosie and B.B.

"I know that voice!" laughs Rocky. "Come on everyone. There's no need to hide."

As the others watch, Rocky and Eddie
pull off all the leaves and pine cones...

... and look, it's only Spike the porcupine! The leaves and pine cones had stuck to his prickles!

"Oh, thank you,"
says Spike. "That feels much
better. I didn't like being a monster!"

CHAPTER SIX

Farmyard Friends

Farmyard Families

If you ever visit Sunny Dale Farm, you will find that it is home to lots of different animal families.

There's Cluck the cockerel and Shirley the hen. They
and their five fluffy, yellow chicks live in the hen
coop in the yard. It's Cluck's job to wake everyone at
sunrise with a loud cockle-doodle-doo!

Rosie the cow lives in the field. She is big, with two
sharp horns growing from her head, but she is very
gentle and kind. She has only one calf and her name
is Ruby. She is named Ruby because her coat is dark
red and it shines in the sunlight like a precious jewel.

Ruby is four weeks old and rarely leaves her mother's side. That is because she needs to drink the milk that Rosie makes for her. The milk will help Ruby to grow into a strong, healthy calf. Soon, she will be old enough to feed on grass and hay as well as milk.

Behind the farmyard is a pond filled with
waterlilies. This is where Lily the white duck
and her three yellow ducklings live. They sleep
in a little wooden house in the middle of the
pond. When they want to go for a swim, the
ducklings slip and slither down the smooth
wooden ramp and land with a splash in the pond.
It's just like a slippery playground slide for ducklings.

Elsie is a mother pig, a sow. She and her piglets, Pip
and Wilf, live in a pig sty. They love their cosy sty.
There's lots of warm, sweet-smelling straw to lie on,
a big squelchy mud bath to roll around in and even

better, there is always lots of food to eat. Every
morning, Farmer John brings buckets of delicious
cereal and vegetables for them to eat! Can you see
who else has come to visit the pigs in their sty?

So now you have met four of the animal families who live at Sunny Dale Farm. There is another family that lives there, too. The animals are soft and furry, with whiskers and a long tail. They love drinking milk and when they're not chasing mice there is nothing they like more than to be curled up asleep on top of a haystack. Look at the picture to see if you can guess which animal family it is.

Lewis Can Do It

"Can't stop to talk. It's harvest time," says
Farmer John. "Today I start to cut down the wheat
with the big yellow tractor."

The rumble and roar of the big yellow tractor's engine frightens the baby animals. The piglets run and hide in the straw and the ducklings bury themselves under Lily's wings. Ruby the calf moves close to Rosie and nestles up against her.

Lewis, the little red tractor is left behind in the field.
He looks very, very sad. He would love to help with
the barvest but Farmer John says that he is too small
to pull the big, heavy harvesting machines.

Lewis watches unhappily as the big yellow tractor rumbles and roars up and down the wheat field, but suddenly all is quiet. The rumble and roar have stopped and the big yellow tractor is not moving.

Farmer John scratches his head. He can't mend the
big yellow tractor and he doesn't know what to do.

"The tractor has broken down," he says miserably.
"How can I finish harvesting before it rains?"

"Lewis can do it," yell all the farmyard animals.

"And I can help, too," says Des the donkey.

Farmer John sits in the seat and starts Lewis' engine.

"Off we go!" shouts Farmer John, and waves.

"Toot! Toot!" whistles Lewis, happily.

"Hee-haw, hee-haw!" cries Des as he trots behind.

All day long, Lewis moves up and down the field cutting the wheat. All day long, Des carries sacks of grain back to the farmyard. It is hard work but Lewis and Des are having a wonderful time!

"Toot! Toot!" whistles Lewis.

"Hee, haw!" cries Des at the top of his voice.

Just as the last stalks of wheat are cut, it begins to rain. Pitter, patter. Pitter, patter.

"Hooray," shouts Farmer John. "We've harvested the wheat in time. Thank you Lewis and Des."

When Lewis and Des come back to the farmyard, all the animals cheer and clap. Lewis is feeling so happy and proud that he starts to blush and turns an even brighter shade of bright red!

Pickles in a Pickle

Farmer John leaned over the fence of the pig sty. "Elsie, I'm going to the market and you're in charge," he says. "Please make sure that no one gets into any mischie while I'm gone."

"Don't worry," says Elsie. "I'll make sure everyone is on their best behaviour."

238

It is a beautiful, sunny day. All the animals are feeling hot and sleepy. Elsie and the other animals in the farmyard settle down to enjoy a lazy day, but Pickles the farm dog doesn't feel at all sleepy. He feels mischievous and full of energy.

"Oh, I'm going to have some fun today!" checkles
Pickles as he runs into the sheep pen, barking and
herding the sheep into a corner.

"Baa, baaa! Baa, baaa!" bleat the frightened sheep.

Elsie hears the bleating and goes to see what's wrong.
But when she gets to the sheep pen, Pickles is
nowhere to be seen and the sheep are quietly feeding.
"That's strange," mutters Elsie, puzzled.

"Now for my next trick," chuckles Pickles, picking up a pawful of stones and hurling them onto the tin roof of the hen coop. The clang, clunk and rattle of the stones on the roof frightens the hens.

"Cluuuuuck, cluck, cluck, cluck, cluuuuck!" squawk the silly hens, running all over the yard.

When Elsie goes to see what's wrong, Pickles is

nowhere to be seen and the hens are quiet.

"That's strange," mutters Elsie, puzzled.

"Now for some real mischief," chuckles Pickles as he carefully climbs onto the old rickety fency around Elsie's sty. In his paw is a long, brown feather. Below him, stretched out in the mud, lies Elsie. She is fast asleep and snoring very loudly.

"Oh, this is going to be lots of fun," thinks Pickles.

But just as Pickles reaches down to tickle Elsie's snout, he leans too far over and loses his balance.

"Whooooooa!!! Help me I'm falling!" yells Pickles as he bellyflops – splat! – into a large puddle of squelchy, slimy, slippery mud.

Can you guess whose turn it is to chuckle now?

Missing Eggs

"Someone has stolen my unhatched chicks!" shrieks
Shirley Hen, running in circles around the farmyard.
"Nonsense," says Elsie. "You've just mislaid them."

"I haven't," says Shirley. "They were in the nest one minute and gone the next. Cluck, cluck, cluck!" While Shirley jumped up and down and flapped her wings with worry, Elsie tried to think what could have happened to the eggs.

"Tell us exactly what happened," says Des.

"Well, when I got up I put some new straw
onto the nest and went to get a drink," says
Shirley. "But when I came back the eggs were gone.
Gone! Cluuuck! Cluuuck!"

Elsie takes charge. She calls all the farm animals
together and orders them to search the farmyard.

"Don't worry, we'll find them," say the animals.

The search goes on all morning. The animals look everywhere but no one finds the missing eggs.

"What do we do now, Elsie?" ask all the animals.

"Everyone be quiet while I think," she replies.

There is silence in the farmyard. Not a sound is
heard until suddenly – cheep, cheep, cheep!
"Did anyone hear a cheep, cheep?" asks Elsie.

The cheeping was coming from Shirley's nest!
As the animals move closer, a little chick
suddenly pops its head up through the straw. This
is followed by another – and another, and another!

"My lovely babies!" cries Shirley. "The thief must
have put the eggs back in the nest!"

"Calm down," says Elsie. "There's no thief. The
eggs weren't stolen, just hidden under the new straw!"